STARSTRUCK MIX-UPS
Here is a clever trick to get you started. Match up the quirky Wally pairs and spot one transformation between them!

First published 2024
by Walker Books Ltd
87 Vauxhall Walk
London SE11 5HJ

2 4 6 8 10 9 7 5 3 1

© 1987–2024 Martin Handford

The right of Martin Handford to be
identified as author of this work has
been asserted in accordance with the
Copyright, Designs and Patents Act 1988

This book has been typeset in
Wallyfont and Optima

Printed in China

British Library Cataloguing in Publication
Data: a catalogue record for this book
is available from the British Library

ISBN 978-1-4063-9703-1

www.walker.co.uk

WALKER BOOKS
AND SUBSIDIARIES
LONDON · BOSTON · SYDNEY · AUCKLAND

WHERE'S WALLY?
THE MIGHTY
MAGICAL
MIX-UP

MARTIN HANDFORD

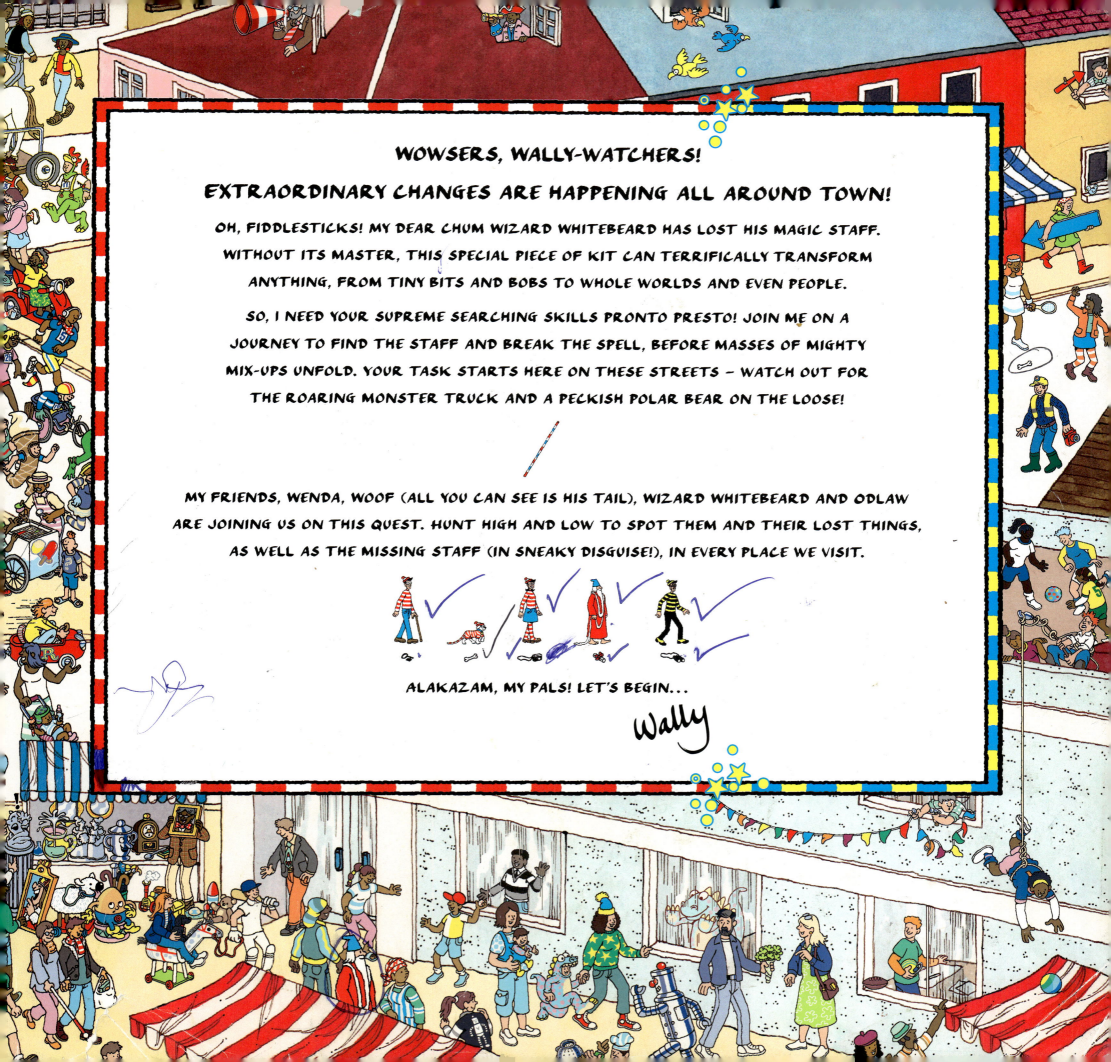

WOWSERS, WALLY-WATCHERS!

EXTRAORDINARY CHANGES ARE HAPPENING ALL AROUND TOWN!

OH, FIDDLESTICKS! MY DEAR CHUM WIZARD WHITEBEARD HAS LOST HIS MAGIC STAFF. WITHOUT ITS MASTER, THIS SPECIAL PIECE OF KIT CAN TERRIFICALLY TRANSFORM ANYTHING, FROM TINY BITS AND BOBS TO WHOLE WORLDS AND EVEN PEOPLE.

SO, I NEED YOUR SUPREME SEARCHING SKILLS PRONTO PRESTO! JOIN ME ON A JOURNEY TO FIND THE STAFF AND BREAK THE SPELL, BEFORE MASSES OF MIGHTY MIX-UPS UNFOLD. YOUR TASK STARTS HERE ON THESE STREETS – WATCH OUT FOR THE ROARING MONSTER TRUCK AND A PECKISH POLAR BEAR ON THE LOOSE!

MY FRIENDS, WENDA, WOOF (ALL YOU CAN SEE IS HIS TAIL), WIZARD WHITEBEARD AND ODLAW ARE JOINING US ON THIS QUEST. HUNT HIGH AND LOW TO SPOT THEM AND THEIR LOST THINGS, AS WELL AS THE MISSING STAFF (IN SNEAKY DISGUISE!), IN EVERY PLACE WE VISIT.

ALAKAZAM, MY PALS! LET'S BEGIN...

Wally

A Sandy Spectacle

Yikes! A baby dragon is hatching on the beach and some *eggs*-traordinary magic is mustering.

A marvellous multiplication spell has been set in motion and now a thunder of dragons is filling the skies.

As the tide turns, can you dig out the sun-shy staff relaxing in the shade? Be sure to watch the puppet show and find four sandcastles too (not including the enormous one!).

MIDNIGHT
AT THE MUSEUM

The crowds have gone home and a
midnight mix-up is tick, tick, ticking
along. History is now raucously real
and wonderfully wide awake! Look
out for puckish portraits and madcap
mummies! Dodge the charging
charioteers and duck the clashing
cutlasses. BOOM, BOOM,
fire the cannons ... it's a
blast in the past!

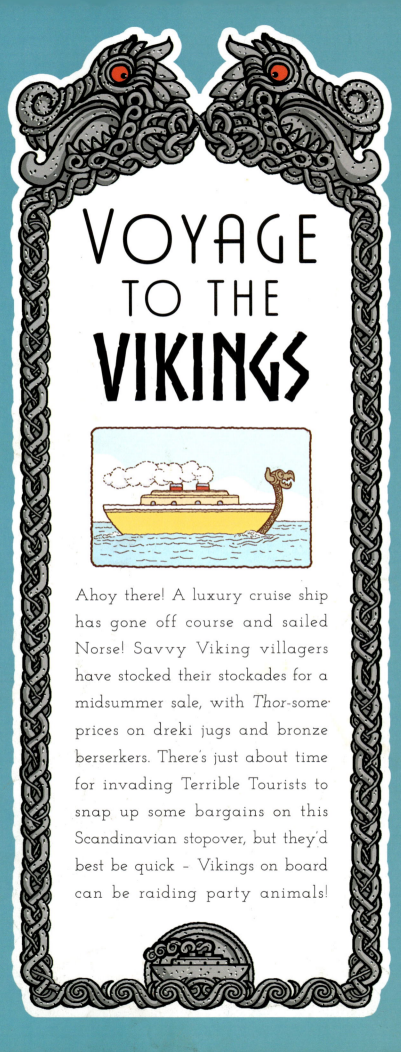

VOYAGE TO THE VIKINGS

Ahoy there! A luxury cruise ship has gone off course and sailed Norse! Savvy Viking villagers have stocked their stockades for a midsummer sale, with *Thor*-some prices on dreki jugs and bronze berserkers. There's just about time for invading Terrible Tourists to snap up some bargains on this Scandinavian stopover, but they'd best be quick – Vikings on board can be raiding party animals!

SPACE AGE

MEETS STONE AGE

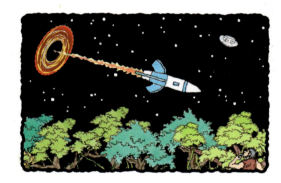

It was a normal Neolithic day of hunter-gathering and washing animal hides when ... CRASHHH! An earth-shuddering thud of heavy metal shook this peaceful world to its craggy core. Alloy aliens clambered from their spacecraft in search of nuts and bolts. Luck's on their side as these Stone Age settlers are happy to swap team-building exercises for tips on wheel-tech wizardry!

* Psst! Woof's bone is near his tail.

CHAOS
IN THE
COLISEUM

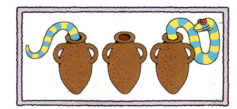

Mighty Maximus! Five
chirpy naiads are filling
the amphitheatre with
water from their enchanted
amphoras. Gutsy gladiators
won't *surf*-ive long in
this colossal circus where
monsters rule the waves. As
you search, watch out for
the ferocious fish devouring
a boat – it rocks! There's
no time for naval-gazing in
this nonsense naumachia!

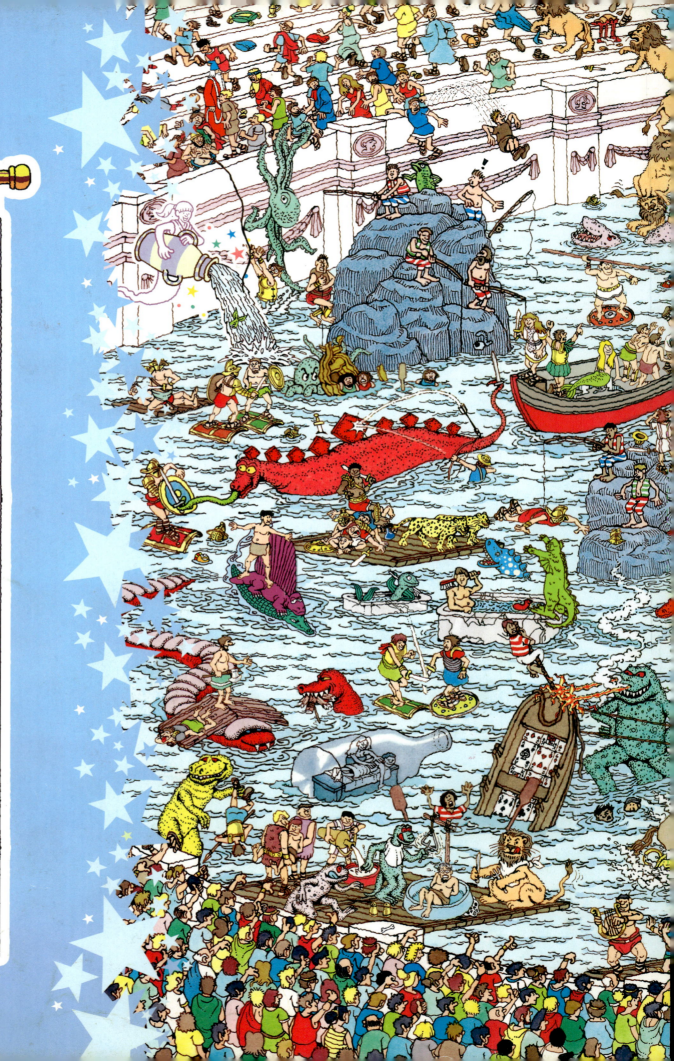

ROBINSON IN BOOTS

THE LAMP LADY

OLIVER OCCHIO

JULIUS CINDERS

A SPELL IN THE LIBRARY

Blazing bluebottles! The staff has been tinkering with the books in Wizard Whitebeard's library and now all the pictures on the spines are muddled up. Luckily the wise wizard made a chart of the real characters earlier! Can you work out who's been mixed up with whom (hint: there are clues in the book titles)? Then, spot two sleuths who have wandered out of their books. Could they be seeking a counter-spell to halt the magical mayhem..?

ATTACK ON CAKE CASTLE

Oh crumbs, the staff has whisked up a truly scrumptious spell! You *knead* to find it quickly as things are a trifle out of hand! Will the brilliant bakers fend off the ravenous raiders before their castle is reduced to a raspberry rubble? When your search is polished off, feast your eyes on the cherry-topped battlements and iced doughnut tower. Yum-yum!

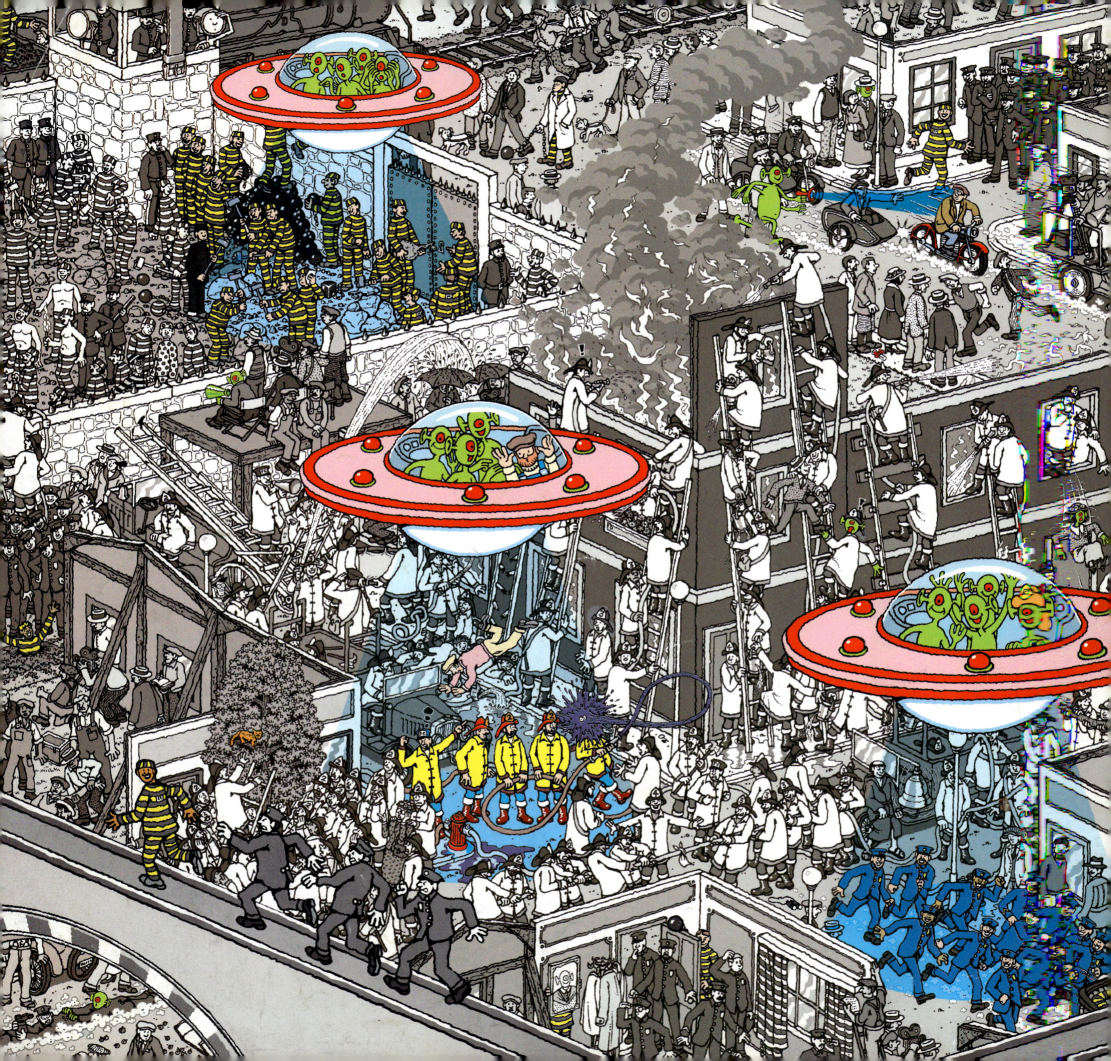

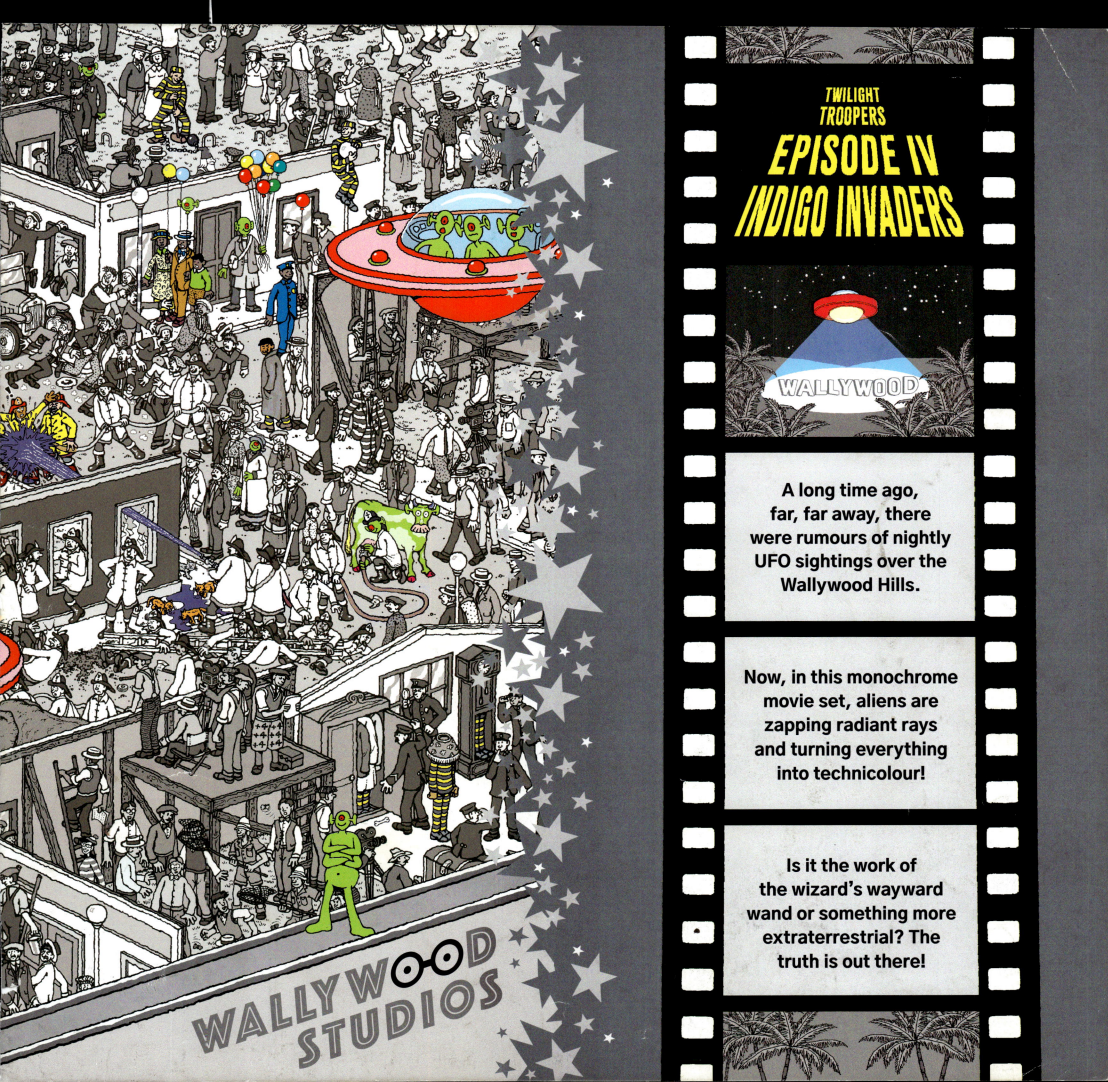

TWILIGHT TROOPERS
EPISODE IV
INDIGO INVADERS

A long time ago,
far, far away, there
were rumours of nightly
UFO sightings over the
Wallywood Hills.

Now, in this monochrome
movie set, aliens are
zapping radiant rays
and turning everything
into technicolour!

Is it the work of
the wizard's wayward
wand or something more
extraterrestrial? The
truth is out there!

WALLYW👓D
STUDIOS

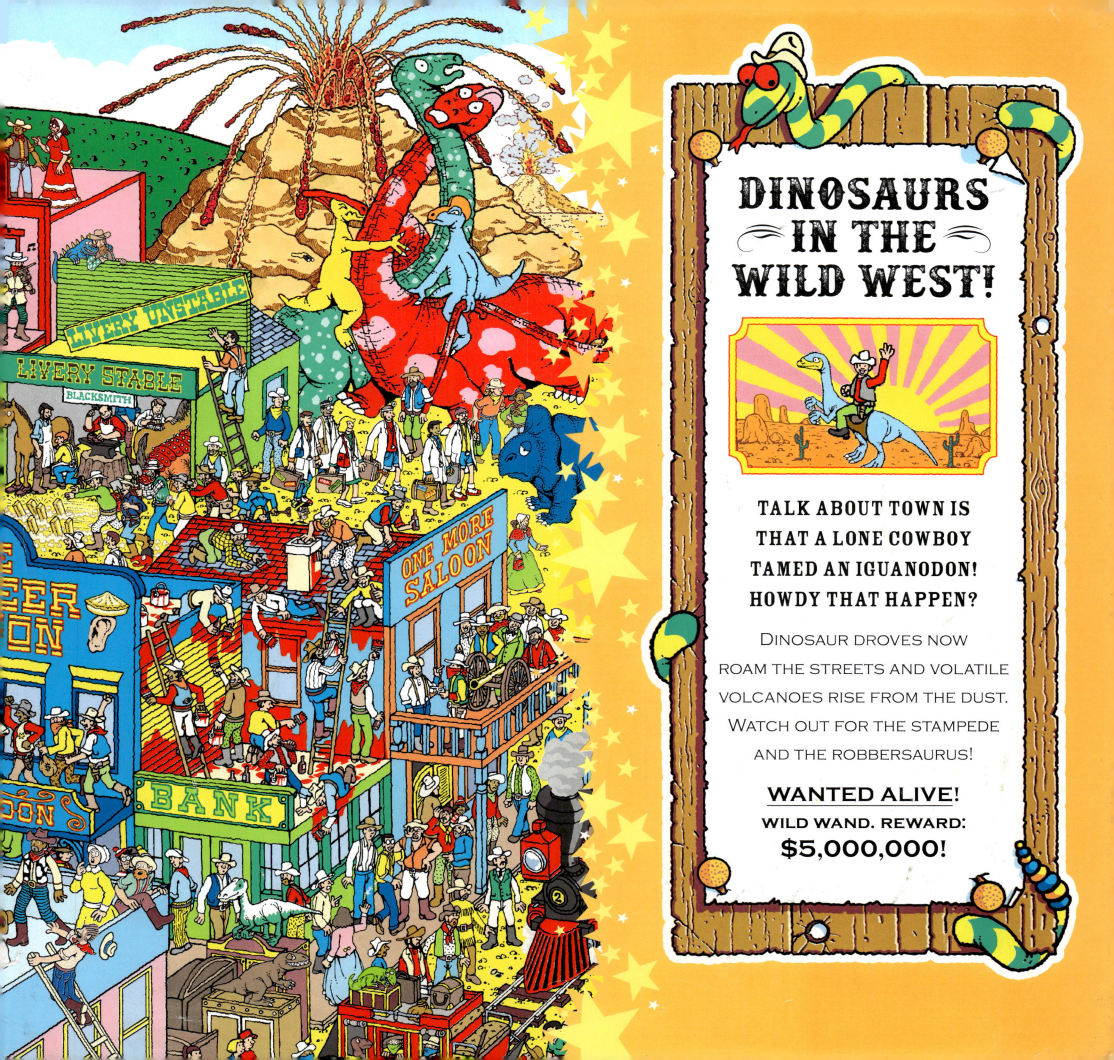

DINOSAURS IN THE WILD WEST!

TALK ABOUT TOWN IS THAT A LONE COWBOY TAMED AN IGUANODON! HOWDY THAT HAPPEN?

Dinosaur droves now roam the streets and volatile volcanoes rise from the dust. Watch out for the stampede and the robbersaurus!

WANTED ALIVE!
WILD WAND. REWARD:
$5,000,000!

FLIGHT TO THE FUTURE

Pelting past Pluto, the zippy staff is spinning through the stratosphere causing a cosmic commotion. A domestic flight has been diverted to 'intergalactic' and time-travelled years into the future. As these dazzled day-trippers get their first taste of space tourism, they need to be wary of the airport workers as something surreal is *Saturn*-ly afoot!

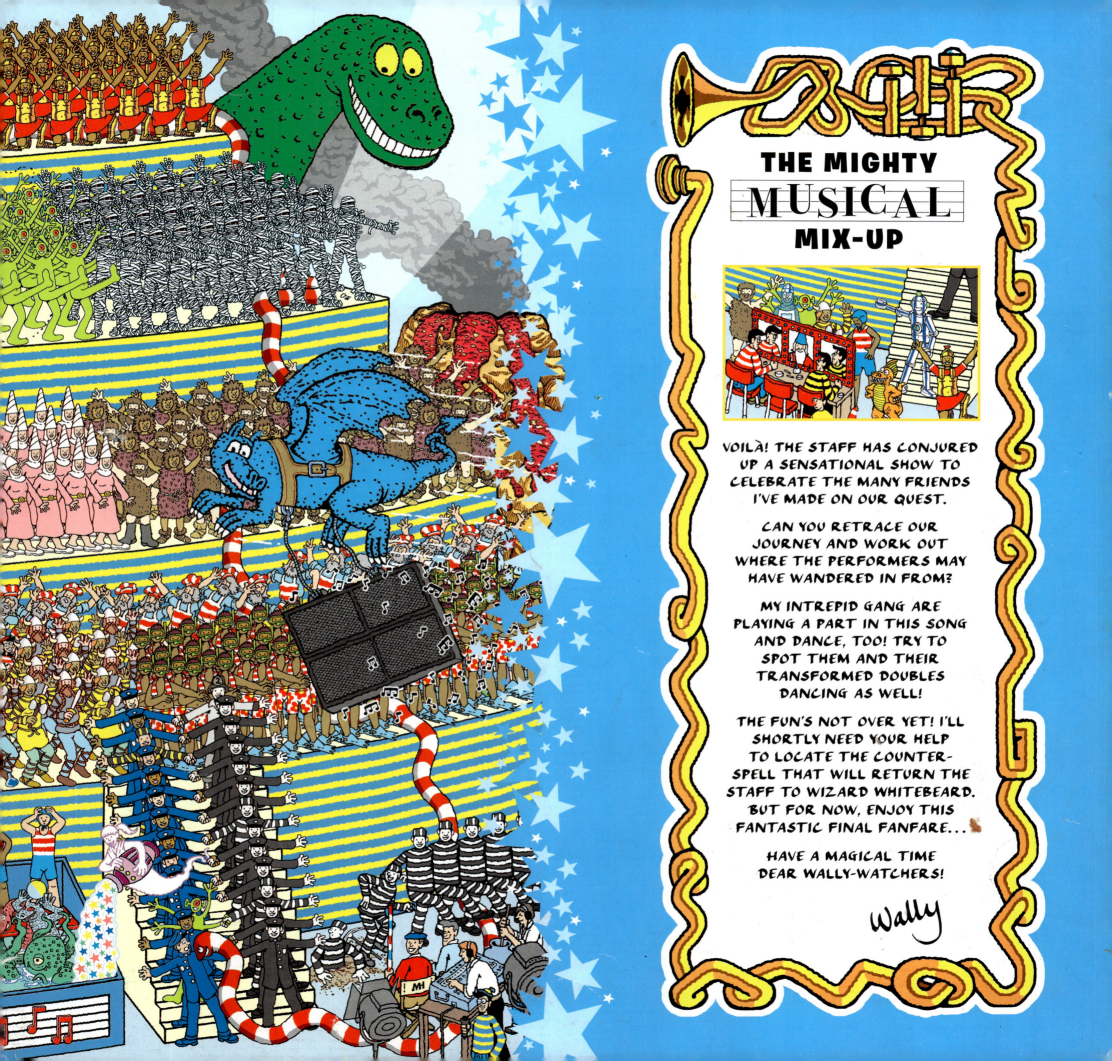

THE MIGHTY MUSICAL MIX-UP

VOILÀ! THE STAFF HAS CONJURED UP A SENSATIONAL SHOW TO CELEBRATE THE MANY FRIENDS I'VE MADE ON OUR QUEST.

CAN YOU RETRACE OUR JOURNEY AND WORK OUT WHERE THE PERFORMERS MAY HAVE WANDERED IN FROM?

MY INTREPID GANG ARE PLAYING A PART IN THIS SONG AND DANCE, TOO! TRY TO SPOT THEM AND THEIR TRANSFORMED DOUBLES DANCING AS WELL!

THE FUN'S NOT OVER YET! I'LL SHORTLY NEED YOUR HELP TO LOCATE THE COUNTER-SPELL THAT WILL RETURN THE STAFF TO WIZARD WHITEBEARD. BUT FOR NOW, ENJOY THIS FANTASTIC FINAL FANFARE...

HAVE A MAGICAL TIME DEAR WALLY-WATCHERS!

Wally

THE MIGHTY MAGICAL MIX-UP! CHECKLISTS

Before the magnificent mayhem is over, have another look through the scenes and search for all the curious things in these checklists.

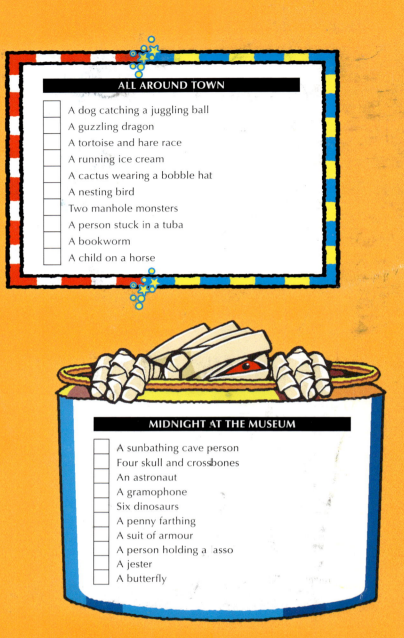

ALL AROUND TOWN

- A dog catching a juggling ball
- A guzzling dragon
- A tortoise and hare race
- A running ice cream
- A cactus wearing a bobble hat
- A nesting bird
- Two manhole monsters
- A person stuck in a tuba
- A bookworm
- A child on a horse

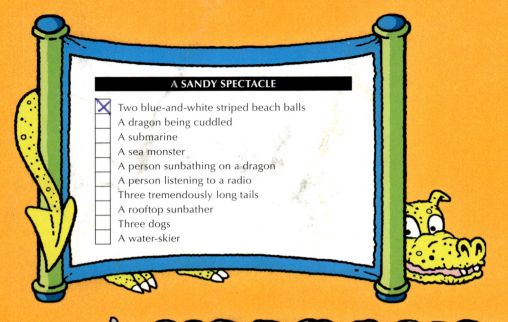

A SANDY SPECTACLE

- [x] Two blue-and-white striped beach balls
- A dragon being cuddled
- A submarine
- A sea monster
- A person sunbathing on a dragon
- A person listening to a radio
- Three tremendously long tails
- A rooftop sunbather
- Three dogs
- A water-skier

MIDNIGHT AT THE MUSEUM

- A sunbathing cave person
- Four skull and crossbones
- An astronaut
- A gramophone
- Six dinosaurs
- A penny farthing
- A suit of armour
- A person holding a lasso
- A jester
- A butterfly

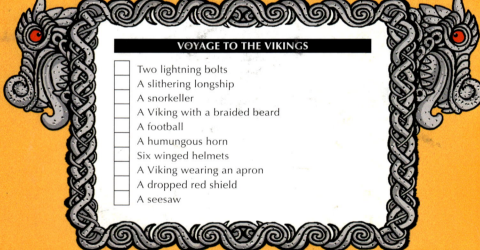

VOYAGE TO THE VIKINGS

- Two lightning bolts
- A slithering longship
- A snorkeller
- A Viking with a braided beard
- A football
- A humungous horn
- Six winged helmets
- A Viking wearing an apron
- A dropped red shield
- A seesaw

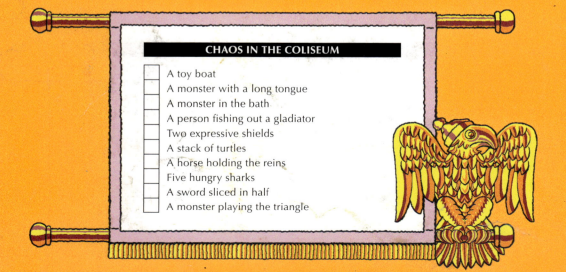

CHAOS IN THE COLISEUM

- A toy boat
- A monster with a long tongue
- A monster in the bath
- A person fishing out a gladiator
- Two expressive shields
- A stack of turtles
- A horse holding the reins
- Five hungry sharks
- A sword sliced in half
- A monster playing the triangle

SPACE AGE MEETS STONE AGE

- A robot rodeo
- A hunting lesson
- A robot reading a map
- A trunk holding a trunk
- A K9 robot
- A robot batting
- Two log boats
- A cow portrait
- Two red apples
- A wild boar chase